Other titles by Wolfgang Hilbig available
from Two Lines Press

The Sleep of the Righteous

Old Rendering Plant

Old Rendering Plant

Wolfgang Hilbig
Translated by Isabel Fargo Cole

TWO LINES
PRESS

Originally published as *Die Weiber*, *Alte Abdeckerei*, *Die Kunde von den Bäumen* by Wolfgang Hilbig, Werke, Erzählungen
© 2010, S. Fischer Verlag GmbH,
Frankfurt am Main

Translation © 2017 by Isabel Fargo Cole

Two Lines Press
582 Market Street, Suite 700, San Francisco, CA 94104
www.twolinespress.com

ISBN 978-1-931883-67-2

Library of Congress Control Number: 2017940026

Cover design by Gabriele Wilson
Cover photo by Christian Richter/Stocksy
Typeset by Jessica Sevey

Printed in the United States of America

1 3 5 7 9 10 8 6 4 2

This project is supported in part by an award from
the National Endowment for the Arts.

ART WORKS.
arts.gov

The translation of this work was supported by a grant from
the Goethe-Institut, which is funded by the German Ministry of
Foreign Affairs.

GOETHE
INSTITUT

Yet in these bounds, these iron walls,
The dreadful portal is unbarred,
Though it stand firm as ancient rock!

— GOETHE

Oystrygods gaggin fishygods

— JAMES JOYCE

I recalled a brook outside town whose current, strangely shimmering, sometimes almost milky, I once followed for miles all autumn or longer, if only hoping to emerge one day from a territory confined, I'll admit it at last, by the bounds of my weariness. And I followed this path as though to the beat of silent wings; when darkness fell, I'd begin to expect some horror, a bloodcurdling cry perhaps, followed by silence…but nothing came, the hush beyond the town and woods was the ceaseless presence of little noises. Farmland, meadows, and fallow fields, swelling up from both sides in the haze of ever-dimmer days, seemed for stretches to throttle the brook to a mere runnel; it often resembled the bluish blade of a long, straight knife slicing the terrain asunder, and the long-drawn wound seemed to steam. — Some distance away, in a hollow, lay the inert eyes of two round forest ponds, their gaze turned inward, half hidden now by dark lids as the shadow of the forest's edge slid over their imperturbable slumber. From there I'd pass through withered cabbage fields on a footpath that turned to follow the brook's course; between this path and the water tall grass grew, the grayed, wildly bristling fall grass of those dim days, obscuring my view of the quick, barely audible runnel. Soon, at almost regular intervals, rotten old pollard willows rose from the grass, and then appeared on the brook's far side as well, standing opposite the intervals between the willows on this side, leaning over, just as these willows reached aslant across the brook's center, so that the branches sprouting from the swollen heads formed a virtual roof above the brook, beneath which, especially when the dusk grew dense, the water's trickling sounded louder, seemed indeed to echo as though in an elongated vault. And when I stopped and listened, I sometimes imagined myself within this canopy of willow boughs, and at times I thought I moved with the current, swaying beneath the black baldachin of willow wands, in a boat of corrosive grief, unfathomably drifting in aimless circles to strand on the shores of another clime entirely. Here the voices of this current had grown to one dense noise, and the other murmurs from the dark that had sealed the evening's end could no longer be heard, though they went on all the same, perhaps as steps across the fields, or as a windy rustling through the leaves, or perhaps as the rolling racket of a distant railroad train, passing on and on as though all night long its trundle and clatter must never break off. Then the water's noise was a trickle, garrulously washing my limbs, rising to flood and shroud me from all the outside things that still sought to infiltrate my weariness. And it was the noise of my weariness as it clamored and frothed…though I was more inclined to suspect a wide-awake scuttling and whispering, sleep-seeking shadows, groping and babbling, when the water washed the willow roots at the channel's edge, when it loosened a stone or handful of dirt from the bank, or grazed trailing grasses and caused the perception of an infinitesimal spraying or hissing, instantly impossible to attend to as it vanished behind me, or fell back behind the next hiss or spray. When I felt the brook carrying the noises away from me, I knew in my heart that I was on the way back, a half-unconscious way back, in a drowsiness I tried to run from but that took shape before me again and again. It was the brook that was running from me… but its run renewed itself ongoing before me, going on to renew its onward rush away from me…and so I stopped at times to make sure the runnel hadn't reversed its flow behind me, or strayed off into a side branch, leaving me behind in total silence: I recalled chasing the water, its noise, for a few quick strides to catch a quickly fading snicker I'd thought I'd seen or heard a moment before… Yet already it had escaped me forever, its memory was swept away forever, and before I knew it the memory of its direction had fled from me in my drowsiness, and with it the direction I had to take back. I strained to hear which way the water flowed: I couldn't determine it, my hearing couldn't orient me as my eyes would easily have done; it was as though the water coursed over me, flowing through my weary brain this way and that, flowing without bounds, as boundless as the railroad noise that ebbed in the distance but could never leave the territory amid which I stood—at the midpoint of that territory that concentrically circled the place where I stood with my eyes shut. Noise upon noise ran stinging in my eyes, and I knew, hurrying onward, that a strange pale-gray haze enveloped me, a cloying breath dried my throat, seemed to hamper my stride, and lay heavy on my face and limbs…and the next afternoon, when I reprised my trek, I thought I sensed the smell still rising from my clothes. For a long time now it had been gathering in my clothes, the clothes I could never change, just as I could not change the earth…for many afternoons now, a smell that aged as I roamed around in it… With seemingly matchless logic I told myself that the smell grew older and older and more tenacious the longer I roamed in it, and that the time would come when at last I could call it my very own smell…if we endured, this smell and I, fused to an amalgam to cover the earth like water. Each afternoon of a certain fall I went this way, more quickly each day, soon without a break, for I knew every step perfectly…recognized nearly every inch, helped by the last light of the late afternoons that were like one single afternoon for me. And after a short time I'd grown used to calling this afternoon way my way back. Tomorrow, I told myself over and over, I'll head back down the same path again, maybe even a crucial bit farther back. — So I fought the dull discontent that beset me each day when I arrived once more at a long-familiar place with no doubt left in my mind that this was where I'd turn around, at this very place, again and again. From this very place began my turn into the night: a place seen so often that it seemed utterly mundane, mundane but not describable: the relevant nouns at my command proved again and again to be treacherous tools, perpetually demonstrating the impotence of all descriptions...compared to the nuances of the visible they seemed, at best, to be sketchy *information*. — At what, for now, was the end of each walk the embankment of a coal train line thoroughly disrupted the already tedious parallel lines of the path, the brook, and the willow rows. The brook passed under the embankment in a tunnel and flowed underground for a stretch, emerging where the terrain fell off in a basin and vanishing into the meadows, branching into a delta of side-channels and ponds, with a few willows left to hint at the bends of its irresolutely unwinding main channel. The path climbed steeply up the railroad embankment, ending at the top as a kind of plateau, or rather merging into a fragment of a road, also elevated, that met the train tracks at a right angle. At first glance the impression was of a random mound of earth, but on closer inspection one made out decayed fragments of concrete foundations, completely overgrown by shrubs and grass, evidently flooded with coal from toppled wagons and mixed with debris from the crumbling pavement; here a roadway had clearly led up to the tracks. I called this rotting concrete foundation, strikingly out of place in the grassy basin, the *ramp*. Up here on the ramp I stopped; at several places along its edge… on the edge of this bridge over the brook…one still saw the stumps of angle irons, the remains of a proper railing, long since scrapped; undeniably, each time I was up here I teetered breathless on the concrete at the edge with no railing and gazed with palpable vertigo into the water flowing several yards below me, shooting swift and slantwise through the vault of the bridge. Muddy grass and dead, bleached shrubs lashed its surface, a hollow gurgling sounded where the water rushed by the slimy stone columns. Up here, as ever, my impression of being utterly without support, without any connection to the images around me, reached its pinnacle: I'd had this impression even mounting the bridge, and once on top I found myself with the certain sense that I'd arisen utterly naked beneath the gray wind-filled sky, that I'd raised myself up beneath the close, bleak clouds that flew apart just above the thrumming overhead lines and, aflutter, were swept off to the east... All at once my surroundings seemed boundlessly astir; the last remnant of the day washed me in breathless weakness, the first evening gloamings clotted below the northern horizon, which the lights in the village houses would soon blot out as they winked on. And it was as though, along with the torrent beneath the bridge, the entire terrain turned in circles beneath me.

It seemed to be some other memory, a memory of much earlier origins, that made me call the bridge's concrete base a ramp…and the sound of the word *ramp* contained, to my ear, some of the indeterminate intensity with which certain severely tarnished terms struggled for more frequent usage; a comparable example was the word *homeland*, on which one set foot as on a train platform, with a sense that nothing bad should be associated with it. — One evening, amid the rapt obsessions of childhood chases and swordplay—I accompanied those games with cries that were meant to be piercing but seemed to fall silent, and what transpired was itself the very end of one such cry—I slipped on the exposed edge of a stone platform and plunged into the empty field of fog. The ragged echo of my voice hung over me; I fell several yards into the silence, fortunately landing on the grass, which grew patchily amid the ruined industrial complexes where I played. It was not the incalculable length of my fall that terrified me but the idea of the clump of matter, invisible in the dusk, on whose slimy slickness I'd lost my footing and helplessly slipped, sliding through it first with my shoe, then with my shin and my knee. Waking from insensate suffocation, I slunk home crestfallen, endured the usual evening reproaches for my tardiness, was sent to bed without closer scrutiny, and, half asleep, dreamed a recurrence of the accident and all the fears in its wake: I could easily have fallen from two or three times that height, I'd been expressly forbidden to go into the ruins, much less alone as I usually did—the prohibition, apparently, was all too justified. No one would have found me: I waged my battles alone against myself, in the ruins, in the hidden corners of those war-ravaged places, where I knew I was safe, unseen and unheard, where I hid my whittled wood sabers, stained green from chopping breaches through the nettles; when the sun set, this green seemed to turn red. Then the shadows lurked in the masonry cracks, waiting for the moment to attack, growing to gigantic size, like the staggered tiers of tin soldiers who seemed to command the whole territory of the windowsill when their long shadows stretched in the moonlight…so too the shadows in the ruins were signs of a never-abating threat, though nothing ever moved in the background, and no attack ever came. When I brandished my saber, these gestures were like a war dance, perhaps my way of warning my adversaries, who confined themselves to observing my maneuvers and remaining under cover: the invisible forms behind the shadows never materialized, the terrain's true possessors never rose up from the underground. — But that changed on the evening of my accident, real figures suddenly staggered across the debris and onto the ramp…real voices grumbled in strange, rolling dialects and grew louder and louder, and I wondered whether the cry I'd heard had really emerged from my throat. I recalled all these things only later, at night; that evening I'd taken them for figments of my imagination, conjured by my constant focus on sword fights in the fog. Now I saw that all my hiding places were exposed, that I was banished, that I'd have to seek other solitary wastelands. But the reason for my swift capitulation came in a dream: I dreamed that I'd been tripped on the ramp by a revolting, slimy deposit underfoot that appalled me in some barely comprehensible way…I shuddered as though I'd touched the naked stuff of death. On waking, I was relieved to ascribe the cause of my disgust to that half-forgotten dream. But no sooner had I risen than the horror caught up with me: my mind faltered as I saw my right leg, my entire calf, covered by a dried mire, a black-green slurry mixed with blood.

Several narrow footpaths ran below the road that led up to the railroad line; darkness was already starting to cover them, like murky waters filling the basin. The paths wound their way to a nearby village, merging into crooked lanes between tumbledown houses that surrounded a bleak marketplace: I knew this, though throughout that autumn I'd never made my way that far. Without admitting it, I was drawn instead to the fence around an old watermill whose grounds lay in the basin's depths. The very first path that turned right from the road would have brought me there; it ended at the gate to the property, which was completely overgrown and surrounded by a ramshackle, almost rotten wooden fence. But even from the gate you couldn't see the mill—I couldn't remember ever having seen it—because the sprawling garden in front of the buildings was choked with

a dense stand of fruit trees and shrubs, an impene-
trable thicket: in the summer one faced a brooding
wall of green as high as a house; in the fall a sea of
yellow fire; and in late fall a barricade, stretching far
back like a leafless jungle behind whose inextricable
tangle the glimmer of a wall was swiftly swallowed
by night's eerily advancing shadows. Sometimes
a window shone out amid the night shadows and
thickets, a lonely glow more forbidding than entic-
ing. — I let my gaze roam farther: the brook rushed
off into a wilderness of still-green nettles as tall as
a man; somewhere, succeeding the willows, poplars
shot upward, the first, it seemed, to lose their leaves
in fall; and soon I saw their branches clad in motionless clumps of blackbirds that met the sundown
with plaintive cries. But perhaps that last image
came from much earlier: from just after the thaw,
when the brook carried more water than one would
have thought possible…when there were no more
nettles, only the poplars rising from the treacherous
swamps and ponds that gradually merged to form
one shining surface. Maybe that was why the lonely
farmstead outside the village was a *watermill* for me:

my memory saw it looming from the dull gray mirror of a watery surface that turned like a millstone, turned faster and faster…and the walls swam, and only the roofs rose above that milling mirror, and soon the whole image was a sourceless reflection beneath the empty orbit of the surface. Baseless, too, was the trepidation—thinking back still further—with which I'd first approached the gate, unsuspecting, yet gripping my new sword, its freshly skinned wood glinting in the sun. I froze; a gigantic black dog had raced silently out of the thickets and hurled itself against the fence slats with frenzied, almost bellowing growls… I woke up, instantly certain that not far from that spot several sections of the fence had fallen over, an opening through which the animal could have pounced; my panic peaked at the notion that the black beast had been strong enough to drag me into the grounds.

Everyone told tales to warn against getting too close to the mill; the darkest one claimed that *foreigners* had settled in the abandoned property, people from Eastern Europe who had ridden out the war here and refused to relinquish their hiding place; as I heard more rumors about them they grew to gigantic stature; they were shifty and violent, aloof and inscrutable—it was said that the farther east you went, the more dangerous the people—and I sensed that in their blind hostility toward the natives they would have failed to see that I myself came from a family whose roots lay far in the east... only the natives saw it, the foreigners saw things differently than people born here. Beyond the tracks of the coal line, to the southeast of a half-deserted village, deep in that wild basin, right behind a rotten fence, began the zone that was the east, and you could not enter this region unpunished. You could not return unpunished to the womb. Everyone knew that people vanished there; no one had ever seen them again, no serious search had been undertaken; in any case they were dubious characters, possessed by quixotic notions and lacking kin. They resembled me in many ways, maybe all of them, too, were eastern by nature; they resembled me but for one final thing: each evening I returned home to my kin. Like a dog, undependable but too tired to stay away, each evening I found myself back in the circle of my family gathered in the lamplight. Those stray figures, though, might have been devoured by the foreigners. Or by the foreigners' outsized curs, by their pigs, by their fish. Or conceivably the foreigners used the vanished youths and maidens as beasts of burden, as draft animals; you could picture them walking under the yoke, harnessed to heavily laden carts with stones piled on top as the coup de grace, driven on by inarticulate cries, animated by a flicking whip, having long since lost all humanity... In the woods one dreaded stumbling upon them: naked creatures that went like animals on all fours and fed on raw meat, runaways who returned to the foreigners' barns of their own accord when winter came. All these imaginings made more sense to me than the pat declaration that this or that person had *vanished* from our sphere; I thought it virtually impossible for someone to vanish in this world, but all the others accepted it with peculiar composure. Undeniably these incidents worried them, but they never asked what they really meant. When someone, a person they might have encountered just a few days before, was suddenly said to have vanished, they never wondered whether this wasn't merely the vaguest possible description of some monstrosity, whether it didn't obfuscate the fact that the fate of the vanished lay in the hands of a power against which none could prevail... I understood it even less when I noticed that the official reports of these incidents never mentioned *vanished people*—they spoke of *seeking missing persons*. For the general public that seemed to make these things all the more abstract: no one seemed to know quite what was being said when someone was *sought* or had *vanished*, whether both meant the same thing, or whether the former determined the latter... After a short while no one said a word about it, as though having reached an understanding that the vanished people had never even existed; when it was said that someone was being sought, this was the final declaration that from that moment on he would never be found. I refused to let this satisfy me—especially since it seemed to violate some prohibition to go on thinking about one of the missing persons, much less talking about him—and was certain that those who had vanished went on existing in some fashion, the proof being that, as I heard, those who still asked after the vanished suddenly went missing as well. The vanished went on existing in the place of disappearance… if I vanished myself someday, this would doubtless be the case, I thought; when I pictured myself vanishing, I went on existing without a break, just in a different territory, within a different state of being, within an unknown reality; and so there was no question that a person dubbed *vanished* had to be thought of as extraordinary, had to be thought of as a better, lost self. Indeed this term was a special title, reason enough for renown—to be a vanished man was to be a legend, to have survived battles that only shadows knew about, transformed into an idea borne onward, which crossed the land like a shadow severed from him who had cast it. Who walked on in people's thoughts, covered up by silence…a silence that lingered in the memory until the next disappearance superseded it. — I'd recall one after another on my way to the coal line, suddenly even remembering their names…and I'd be haunted by the thought that the territory of their disappearance began just beyond the coal line. And I'd wonder, oddly enough always just as I returned to town, if I hadn't joined the vanished myself, if the shadowy renown of silence hadn't come to cover my name as well. I wondered this whenever the streets just inside the town, so familiar to me, had me groping as if through a tangled labyrinth, whenever I had to admit I might as well be back on the crooked lanes of an abandoned village beyond the coal line, or back in earlier times, in the rubble fields of the bombed-out factories where I was forbidden to go. It was a kind of self-oblivion that made it easy to say whatever came to mind when asked where I'd been. Effortlessly I made up the most tortuous tales without considering myself too bald-faced a liar, for I truly seemed to lack any recollection of my afternoon existence: all the tales I invented were mere variations on my mode of vanishing. Of course no one believed me, but I went on lying doggedly, so that at last—once I learned to ignore all the tension and disregard even the irate reactions to my behavior—nearly every form of communication between my relatives and myself died out and I achieved a relationship describable as a type of grim tolerance, a state in which I truly felt like someone who had vanished from our sphere. And indeed I never ceased to suspect that my senses were tricking me when, each evening, I found myself returning, much too late for my age...so consistently late, to boot, that my tardiness could not be called accidental... When I saw myself turn up at the apartment long past dinner, I entered a silence it seemed forbidden to break, in which I moved as though invisible, like someone who could go on pursuing his fantasies in peace, who occupied, unobserved, certain desolated corners of the rooms, filling them with voices that went unheard beneath a dusty layer of silence.

On the rare occasions when they even noticed my entrance, it did not seem entirely unexpected... the adults' monosyllabic unease, as they sat at the table with their plates already pushed to the middle, seemed to be caused by the startling presence of an uncanny and irksome though barely visible intruder: some strange guest, a close-lipped, ghostly boy, acting as though he'd been here for ages, had stepped forward to poke at what was left of dinner; an apparition, a phantom, an annoyingly obtrusive spirit

whom they hoped each evening to be rid of, yet
who, like some evil curse, would not leave this un-
happy family in peace. — My senses were already
tricked when, having left behind the forest and the
allotment gardens outside town, I turned a corner
and stepped into the pool of light cast by the lamp
directly opposite our house...weren't these univer-
sally familiar sensations, which everyone claimed to
know, mere sensory illusions, wasn't it in fact highly
peculiar that this street seemed so recognizable simply because I had been born there? Wasn't it suspi-
cious that my perceptions guided me so unerringly
that they always triggered the same reflexes? Later I
avoided coming too close to our front door—so that
my faintheartedness would not make me open it, or
because there was no reason to do anything else but
go through it, go up into the center of my weariness;
faced with this door I had no other option than to
unlock it with the key I'd carried for twenty-five
years in my left-hand jacket pocket, dreading the
end of the few steps that led to the second floor,
climbing them haltingly and mechanically, always
poised to turn back...to rush down the stairs as

though ambushed at the top by a growling black beast at the very moment when the timed light went out again, like the moment of gathering darkness behind an invitingly toppled fence…or to start back simply because the light put me at risk of extinguishing my disappearance, of reducing myself to the self predetermined for me, that wretched *I* living in expectation of the whole gigantic burden of the future in which it would be hopelessly trapped. I regularly fled down a side street, giving our house a wide berth, and headed into town. But though my hostility toward the abhorrent town center outweighed my distaste for the moment when, conspicuously befuddled and bedraggled, I'd have to step into the bright light of our apartment, nothing seemed more impossible than an honest account of my whereabouts that afternoon and evening. Given that even in my earliest childhood I'd had no explanation for being late to all activities regarded as essential, what should I have replied, later on, to the increasingly feeble inquiries into the daily vanishing act that made me an extremely rare apparition at home: Should I have said that it was too late to know the reasons…too late to abandon the early years and dark times without endangering body and soul? And how could I have conveyed that I couldn't forego the experience of the hour that most entranced me: the hour of transition, when boundlessness held sway before the onset of night, expressed in barely perceptible overlays of radiance, manifested in unreal hues and noises whose causes were lost… in smells released by changing temperatures, from fissures and shifts in the crusts that seemed to seal off the visible surfaces… I couldn't bear to miss the hour when unknown life, rumored to be dead, crept out under the shelter of the shadows, crept out in the hour of the shadows that wandered across the world to obscure it from the eye, in the hour of the obscuring shadows that hid in the grave of the night, in the hour when the vanished began their day, in the hour when I became invisible, guided only by scents whose signals no longer brushed my brain, but coursed from my senses straight to my limbs… at that half-time when I learned to express myself in whispers, to think with the dead and the banished, with unsubstantial things, with soils, with stones and rivers, with the speechless, soundless animal beings hostile to humanity. It was the hour when some dark utterance waxed within me, needing no words, no names, no logical thoughts...a language in which the nouns lost their meaning, the language of an awareness that responded only to wordless, fleeting moments, made from the nameless sensations of the breath that quickened my blood or made it pulse more strongly, and slowed my stride or lent it lightness, so that it seemed to vault over imperceptible shifts in the air, or sink through sloping zones of warmth hidden by the haze of the discoloring plain...far more than that, this language was an instinctual response to toppled boundaries, an unthinking grasp of light and dark, a capricious certainty in the soles of my feet when venturing one delicate step from the certain to the uncertain. — Of what should I have spoken...? That a nocturnal gleam of light had made me pay the price of lingering too long, a veil of light that a moment later was nothingness, impossible to pin down with nouns, impossible to convey by logic...? What was a serendipitous term from the shadow realm of descriptions: shooting star, bat? What had made that gleam flit through the willows' night-branches? Should I have said that I was bound solely to an hour that enveloped me like an imaginary pelt, shot through with electrified nerves that teased apart the fibers of the dark air in which I walked safely, for the vapor from my nostrils sent intuitions on ahead of me, intuitions of which I was otherwise incapable? — No sooner had my eyes learned to see—and I could learn to see only in the dark—than I found myself transported back to our apartment's world of objects. But I knew I still remained in the pallid swath between two dark masses in whose gloom the willows abruptly turned to bare poplars, and where the ridge of the coal line sliced an obliterating diagonal through the flux of atmospheres…I knew my steps still paced the fields—hounded steps I heard with the look of a hounded man…I still heard the distant, encircling trundle of the trains, the distant, skyward-flickering din of expanding infinitude, a roar of iron that retreat and distance pulverized and gusts of wind swept away, and then again the trundling, a trundling noise that dogged me as I hastened through weariness. And perhaps it was the brook that began to encircle me with its snickers and whispers, from which jarring voices trundled like a mockery of all nouns, and of all adjectives, which I could hear shattering on my face…with a menacing murmur when, like the night, it left its ancestral banks to flow far over the land until nothing could be seen but a spectral row of willows—filing eastward and about to topple, followed by a few bare poplars—and a lonely farmstead behind the railroad's black embankment with a single window like a yellow fang, staring up amid slumped thickets from a sheet of water in which scraps of moon were mirrored. — Oh…never again, I'd promised myself, should I be sent to bed, as in the old days, while the evening was still bright. I could avoid it by staying out until it got dark: all the summers of my childhood were a protracted punishment for my incorrigible lying, and I constantly yearned for the fall, for November, fog, age, weariness, dark. I feared the nights spent half in a sun-flooded chamber, when I couldn't fall asleep until the first shadows filled the room. Once the twilight grew too dense to keep my lids open beneath its weight, the light of the single streetlight across the street, just at the height of my window, would go on with a shock I fancied I could hear and flood the ceiling with a milk-white glow in which a pale pink core of flame seemed to tremble; now, from the intersection with the side street by my window, a car with glaring headlights would turn onto our street, making a glowing wedge of light circle the ceiling, and the streetlight, its color momentarily suffused with that of the headlights, would flare up in such a blaze that each night, torn from my doze by the roar of the motor, I recalled the fires from the air raids that had raged in our neighborhood. Once the beam of the headlights vanished, a black geometric figure shaped like a gigantic cleaver—I took it for the shadow of an advertising column which the car had to pass—moved in the opposite direction from the window across the ceiling, gliding through the room with a casual flourish, a razor slash from left to right, from nape to front, for I, in nightly anticipation of its appearance, was incapable of turning to my other side. The blow came with what was clearly an executioner's precision, smoothly, silently slicing off the ceiling, and once the blade melted away again, I thought I was lying beneath the open sky, beneath tiny, glittering summer stars…I'd heard neither a sawing nor a tearing as if the curtain had been cut, the curtain that billowed for a moment and then sank back, instead I'd heard an impact, a far faint noise, dully swallowed by a shrill dream-cry's cottony echo: a head plummeting into the dream that recurred with that terrified sound; or the thud of a decapitated body, the dull sound with which the dream broke off in that body as it collapsed onto something soft, like the depression in the bed in which I floated; or like a basket beneath a dark and ruinous scaffold of catastrophic geometries resembling social orders embodied, through which the mad heavens trailed thin, noisomely trickling runnels, drawn thin between the executive and the legislative… It was some time before I identified the thud as the slamming of a car door nearby, the same car I'd just heard, which parked on our street every evening but had long since left by morning, when I tried to verify its existence on my way to school…an indefinable car, covered in dull gray-green paint, resembling a delivery van, with a box-shaped body whose back doors had two blind windows of wired glass: It's off on its shuttle trips, I thought in the morning, they start early and don't end until nightfall, so the summer is the time of most traffic, to and fro between the region of the vanished and the towns of those who haven't vanished yet. The nights, the lulls in this traffic, are especially short in summer: and in fall and winter no one vanishes, such a thing is unheard of. In the winter there's nothing but announcements of missing persons. At last the car stands idle on our street, the street I won't recognize till morning... and lacking the strength to persuade myself that my perceptions had more harmless causes, I drifted out onto sleep's vast, somber field, lured by rushing and flowing: the brook that surged up louder and louder, its clamor flooding unimpeded over the walls of the room...the roof was swept away, the stars' lofty, toxic lights spun as though seen through maelstroms. While I sank deeper and deeper, the objects surrounding me grew more and more vague; only far above, in the most remote heights, could I still see dizzying clarity; the moonlight shifted its weak reflection upon the lumpy mass of my pillow, I saw it from the corner of my eye, and glimpsed the pale fog that had settled over the brook…vividly I recalled its pungent sweetness that aroused impervious dread, that seemed to fill my eyes completely with its damp blue luminescence, and I preferred to rest my gaze on the dark wool blanket wrapped tightly around me: I favored this blanket until deep in the cold fall, claiming the duvet was too warm… in reality I feared I wouldn't fall asleep in the brightness diffused by the covers' white cloth. But I'd long since come to rest in the streambed…eyes still open, I thought I was falling asleep at last, saw, still asleep, the perplexingly fog-filled region through which the stream carried me; one moment mildly warm water seemed to envelop my limbs, and above I saw the round immobile moon beneath which I rapidly drifted…but then the full moon was torn to shreds, I couldn't tell what was swept along beneath it, clouds or water whose surface closed icily over my face. The next moment I was wide awake, my mind endowed with lucid thoughts: I saw that I was long since on my way again, my way alongside the brook, long since on my way back to the mill. And I suddenly sensed the nature of the terrain on which I walked: it was hardly solid ground…and perhaps what I walked on couldn't even be called earth, this matter that buckled beneath my steps and sometimes seemed to sigh from its depths with a hollow reverberation. Hadn't the term *earth* arisen solely on the basis of an embarrassed convention, wasn't it a noun that passed in silence over matter's true nature…? Wasn't the use of substantive nouns nearly always a silence about the true substances of things—and wasn't that silence so essential to us that it became the basic material of our thinking? What were we really passing over: over silenced things, over vanished things, over the basic substance of ourselves, over the silence in our thoughts? Passing silently over our silence…? I sensed it as an elastic tension underfoot, twitching now and then, sometimes I seemed to hasten forward over tensely listening eardrums…flesh smacked under me; when my tardy steps touched the earth I seemed to feel it, juices dispersing beneath me as I forced myself into

an insouciant saunter. It was as though someone, a
long shadow, were walking ahead of me, and I had
to put on a show of assurance…assurance: one time
my foot sank into some sort of viscous sludge, and
when I tried to escape, there were more puddles,
seeming to congeal. I nearly slipped, the slope of the
bank invisible before me, mist-cloaked delusion and
incoherent trickling…then level ground once more,
stretches where a scabby crust crunched, solidified,
already turning into dust, into a strange snow…
dying into a strange snow I stirred up in caustic
swirls, and I blew my nose, a loud, resounding honk,
then stumbled on hastily. Now I saw a sheen on
the ground, gray-white and powdery, a loose sediment gathered softly in the hollows; it flew up
when I jumped across with a single terrified ex-
clamation I wouldn't remember later…loud and
resounding, so that I heard it far ahead of me, far
ahead of me someone heard it; residue from the
mist billowed over the brook's channel, swirls of
strange dust or meal milled from the water's va-
porous brew settled once more as pale precipitation amid the grasses: and I stirred it up as I

walked, quickening my pace to pass through the mists that swallowed a long dark shadow before me, a shadow that swirled the dust… Billows flew in my face; a sifting; a shimmering like the pale vapors of my sheets in the shadowy bedroom; a numbingly sweet trickling; the taste of the malodorous twilight, billowing clouds like milk-colored gas, dully attacking the eardrums of my consciousness…until all at once I was empty and in front of me was a form, spectral as the compacted mist I swallowed, a form I saw hasten along the brook's edge and plunge into the sharp shadow of the embankment, vanishing. Empty and filled with indistinct fear I stood for some time, still hidden by the sifting vapors that tasted like soap…before me lay the dark boundary, the rampart through which the brook escaped, and with it the form that had gone ahead of me, the youthful silhouette of my imagination that I had vainly awaited on the crest of the embankment. It hadn't appeared, I'd lost the child of my thoughts at the top of the ramp whose blackness now faced me; nothing but a rough noise, a honk or a cry, seemed to flee up above, heading toward the eastern sky whose pale gray grinned at me.

Never would I leave the place where I lived. — Even before reaching the last part of my route, before that dead stretch of concrete debris and burned tar, I turned back, turning the empty body of my weariness, failing as always, and started homeward, toward the midpoint which, from weariness, home was professed to be, to the center that was our house on our street—this being the most detached description I could think of—under the light on our street, encircled by the debris of noise carried up by lurching winds, to the house that was the midpoint of all voices, surrounded by all the news that rushed up through the ether, hemmed in by the sonorous trundling of the reports, the names, the titles, the substances infiltrating all the corners of this apartment, creeping like dry rot into the walls, depositing sediment on all things, making all matter billow like moonlight, like mist; and trickling from all the cracks like swarms of ants scuttling over paper, like monotonous insects flying across tables and sills, missing person announcements smoking up like smells from the hearths and like a rain of sweat and blood from the coal.

Only once in my life had I attempted, all the same, to leave the circle of my kin, the place where I lived, the house in whose rooms the news reports converged like water, for a few days, no more, to visit a friend up north. A peculiar incident haunted my days in the north and ultimately chased me back, though my intent had been to stay. Afterward, as usual, I described the event to myself as a dream, but now I would never quite be sure: on the very first evening, arriving late at night—in a dream, I told myself—I groped my way across the unlit entry hall toward the first step, and stepped on an object, a fat, bloated object that burst audibly underfoot. Instantly a stench swelled up, the floor was slippery, the stench so appalling that, holding my breath, I dashed up the stairs in a panic and didn't breathe again until the door of my friend's apartment slammed shut behind me. In my dream I was convinced I'd stepped on a dead rat in the dark; the bulging corpse of a drowned water rat, I told myself, ice-cold in my dream… When I woke up the next morning, memory delivered me: I'd arrived by daylight, my friend greeting me from the second-story window, and a moment later we'd stood in the sun-flooded entry hall while I admired the beautifully painted porcelain tiles that covered the walls to the height of the banister. After the dream, though, I couldn't enjoy my breakfast, thinking of the burst of stench that still rang in my ears. Finally, shaking my head, I went out to the stairwell and looked over the banister. Who could describe my horror when I saw that I hadn't been dreaming, or that I'd dreamed what was true: down in the hall lay the ruptured cadaver of an enormous rat, staring at me with jaws agape, as though it had just uttered a plaintive cry...and as though that cry had summoned me, our gazes plunged together for one hate-filled moment. When my friend came back from work that afternoon I didn't dare mention the incident; he didn't speak of it either, so I assumed that the dead creature had been removed...but I couldn't forget the beast's gaze, and didn't feel better until, several days later, I startled my friend with the decision to leave.

It was the fear of that same stench—or so I constantly told myself—that kept me from crossing the railroad embankment, or even reaching it, and perhaps this was the truth. I had no idea how I'd managed to ignore the smell. At any rate, earlier on in my childhood years, I had known it very well. I'd known it to dog my footsteps every day, especially in the evening, after dark, especially in the last weeks of summer and through the autumn months. It was transported by the brook from one of the disorienting, seemingly endless outskirts where desolate stretches of fallow land kept giving way to unexpected enclaves and enigmatic industrial areas. As a child I knew it was the smell of the milk-colored current that washed down the brook, bubbling and steaming like warm soapsuds in the evening. I knew that the smell soaked the banks and seeped under the fields; the mist over the river channel was this smell, and that mist rose from the topsoil too, infecting everything that grew in the fields, and it rose from the meadows, the grass of the paddocks smelled of the river mist's cloying essence, the bushes on the banks thrived amid this smell, a smell of flesh...old, useless flesh, relinquished to the water, washed its smell through the land to the east, I knew this as a child. Tallow sheathed the snarls of grass on the brook's edge, ancient fat clung indelibly to the slopes of the embankment; it was a brew of rancid fatback, even covering the paths, boiled-out horns, bones cooked to the point of disintegration…the old river-willows luxuriated in this nourishment; countless bluebottles, ill from overfeeding, dripping like glossy shapes made of wax, skimmed sluggishly through the foam, and this shimmering foam, rapidly turning black, spun lazily on the water by the willows' dangling roots. In truth, when it was still light on my way back to the mill, hadn't my unerring childish eyes spotted indefinable fibers and clumps in the water; hadn't I thought I saw scraps of skin still covered with bristles and dissolving shreds of flesh drifting in the slime and fatty white-yellow broth…? On my way home, when I could no longer see a thing, I had to keep from getting too close to the water; with revulsion I recalled swimming through that liquor in a dream, amid a pulp of organic residues cooked to the point of collapse, barely neutralized by some sort of soap whose cloying glycerin solution seemed to unduly speed the current of the almost seething water. And I could not get too close to the old willows that sweated out the oils from the meats they fed upon...I could not impinge on the circle of their immoderate metabolism; I could not touch them, *the old renderer's willows* leaking phosphorescent ptomaine from the lancets of their leaves, for they thrived without cease: the death of the fauna made them grow strong, potent enough to overwinter in their black-green luster. While the other plants along the watercourse looked sickly and surfeited—all the vegetation struck me as corpulent and phlegmatic, overfertilized and overbred, its natural processes strangely retarded in the fall, when the foliage looked fatter than usual and seemed to eat its way rampantly onward, though its dark green looked so dull and unclean that I expected to see it collapse at any moment—I thought I could see the willows devolving into unheard-of wildness: in the twilight, when the mist rose ever denser from the bank, they seemed to metamorphose into fantastic creatures, the spawn of some freakishly fertile subsoil, ugly crippled excrescences that through their very degeneration had come into power and evil. I saw shapes in them like grimacing faces, not quite identifiable as vegetation, nor as any species of animal I knew; their expressions had something strangely skulking, and they seemed ever ready to pull up, like worms from the mud, the roots that held them so unreliably and shamble many-footed along the course of the waters that were both nourishment and death for them…in this contorted skulking and in their eldritch age was a spectral dignity, like that of invalids hobbling through weird tales, creaking and gray in their craftiness…thus they seemed filled with abilities beyond their due, and like monstrous creatures long believed extinct they seemed gifted with supernatural senses that called into question the very death whose proximity bowed them down. In the mist that scudded around them in the dusk and in the darkness, the character of their grimaces altered perpetually: first I would see them rigid with pain, mortal fear crippling them, and it wouldn't have surprised me if audible laments had coursed from their bristled heads; but suddenly, when they glimpsed me, their branches began to whisper and sigh, sounding like a wondrous enticement; and at last it was sudden rage, clear even in the gathering darkness, and in a frenzy they banded together to cover the noxious night-stream that swelled between them, to shelter it protectively as though it were the elixir of their moribund existence, the secret spring of their dark power and the true serpents' nest of the roots that hindered their fall. When the least breath of air reached them, they seemed in imminent danger, and a commotion passed through the night-world around the renderers' willows: they united in a conspiratorial phalanx, merged to form a barricade, whispering as though constantly counting and calculating, and strange beams of light seemed to dart to and fro before the solid wall of their trunks, which for all their rigid postures concealed an unexpected suppleness. Heavy, drawn-out breathing had set in over the ground's sluggish warmth, like the greedy gasping of corpses stirred from their rest beneath all the surfaces of earth and water, and when the brook made its runnel rise under the milky vapors of this breath, the willows' mask-like faces twitched with a grin that turned to stone around the dawn, congealed and egocentric, and as rough as the dry-damp rock gray of crustaceans from prehistoric oceans.

Far away, the railroad trundled…perpetual evacuation of vanished existence, I whispered… perpetually the arrayed axles of an unheard-of steel world droned, pulverizing every stirring of huddled life…while the beastly land around me called forth the hideous truths of an underworld that began just inches beneath the grass…grass over which there was always something roaming, an invisible man's ceaseless stride, a breathless man's throttled gait, a child's hasty flight…and over that a flutter of wings, making a layer of the dark air suddenly swirl in vortices, silent vortices as though a shadow had swiftly winged upward with an invisible silent soughing in the dark air to settle in the boughs of the willows, fluttering on in the boughs of the willows whose horns gored the darkness and seemed to shake it angrily, to lend it wings…and over that a few stars, flashing momentarily over the somber cloud-sails' silent race, momentarily seeming to race themselves, winged, before vanishing back into the palls of the cloud-mists…and over the moments of these stars' lights was the rushing void of space. The rushing void of time…while far away in the brown smolder of the eastern horizon, dead poplars reared up, plaintive verticals whose unalleviated prominence menacingly abjured the fading night like crucifixes whose arms had been hacked from their trunks.

And I saw with alarm that I had finally lost all acceptable sense of lateness…ah, that in the end it was an entire night too late, that the childhood of my lateness was over: and so I was no longer asked where I had been. So I was finally forced to step *as an adult* through the now-narrow door into the circle of light where the silent, fearful elders sat. Ah, for decades now I'd lived among them, a child, irresponsible and mendacious, muttering childish excuses in an unpracticed singsong, always after dark, with a dwarf's guilty look amid their mute disapproval, and always I'd obeyed them, though wondering at their admonitions, and hadn't dared to turn one last time to my toys, to turn so late to the wooden horses whose headless riders thrust aloft the shafts of stateless banners beneath the Christmas tree stars, which I collected so that in summer, during the too-short nights when I never glimpsed the real stars, I could decorate the dull green of my flowerpots: then night loomed over the blossoms, then even by day a wondrous cosmos revolved over the perpetually green stalks on the windowsill, and under their broad leaves the tin soldiers I had molded myself lay in ambush, the fainthearted fighters of, by now, a more than thirty years' war. Too late for them to reemerge from cover, where they waited tirelessly for a foe, for some old indefinable evil advancing from unknown regions…on the march through ruins long since bullet-riddled, advancing by night behind the fog, while the advance guard already rested in the shelter of the brook-willows, the gleam of their fires stealing moon-hued through the branches and shining across the water: for years now my way back had been cut off.

I recalled setting out on the way back all the same, on into my dreams, dressed in the knee-length shorts that barely fit over my thighs anymore, setting out from fear of the evening news, from fear of appearing, with my most mundane of all names, in the evening list of missing persons, which, broken by funeral marches and polka strains, ebbed through the kitchen and suddenly, in the lamp's agitated glimmer, threw into relief all the incompetence of the bleak furniture that no longer stood where it was supposed to and whose shadows no longer hid my secret corner... Oh, those homeward journeys, laughable enough in the snow-white knee socks I'd already soiled on the shores of the ash fields on the way out, in the fields where the withered cabbage grew, scorched by affliction, after the sun had died out in the eyes of the ponds, asleep beneath the lids of the woods, already dreaming myself on the ash fields: anything not to be responsible. I recalled how I scarcely dared to come home, dressed in the short sailor shirt that no longer closed over my hairy chest but that I pretended to like all the same; how I waited, shivering at the end of the street in the desolate darkness, until I felt the nightmarish alphabet had been recited far enough, until the streetlights, switching on at approximately the letter *P*, gave me the sign, and

I darted unseen through the light to the front door.

For decades, in defiance of frantic remonstrations and warnings, I had persistently stayed out until after the evening news on the radio, managing with some precision to correlate the beginning and end of the news and the sequence of the subsequent broadcasts with the seasonal light conditions; I knew our streetlight switched on much too late in the winter and much too early in the summer—after the eight-o'clock news in winter and during the ten-o'clock news in summer, meaning that in summer I never heard the missing person announcements. But in winter, every night and for many years, I was lulled to sleep by the announcer's tireless voice, whose cadence never changed. To punish my lateness I'd been sent to bed without dinner...or I'd been sent to bed so as not to be a nuisance during the news, for which the kitchen had to be dead silent...and I absorbed the monotonous recital of endless alphabetical lists of names; I pictured how the endless lines of dry names with their scant distinguishing features would curl under the kitchen lamp, turning and forming spirals like eddies, nothing escaping those snares but shy whispers; the recital never paused, seeping through my room's closed door in the dull sloshing rhythm of an increasingly indistinct groundswell of letters, and I heard the breath of silence from the adults' half-open mouths accompanying the wash of those waves like a noiseless breeze that failed to find its course over the sonorous sea of vowels and consonants…for more than ten years I'd been waiting for a sigh, a breath catching in the kitchen to tell me that the listened-for name had been said: my name. All this time the name had failed to come, remained missing…all this time other names murmured away at me, similar, barely distinguishable names, identical names that bored and sapped me, following me into my dreams to bring void and vertigo—but I knew they were still there when I woke, studding the ceiling, fading only for seconds in the darts of light that shot through the curtains, giving me a second's time to fall asleep with a sonorous sawing that scarcely differed from the sawing and rasping of the names…rasping like small but assiduous waves on the shore, trickling up to the far-too-large adult bed in which I lay crosswise and head down in a swaying, spinning voyage beneath the twilight of letters impossible to dim as, beneath the moon's burning baby-face, I drifted out on the empty, watery fields of my dreams: *…seeking Schiller, Frank… Schiller, Franz…Schiller, Franz Heinrich…Schiller, Franz Otto…Schiller, Friedrich…seeking Schiller, Fritz… Schiller, Gustav…* My dreams left the adults' morose perplexity behind, left it behind in the fermented night air of the town, where a dull prudence prevailed amid which my childish soul was a fiend of falsehood. Now the night was past, and I could stop speaking in a childlike falsetto; freed from that existence that had lasted twenty or thirty years, it was time for me to enter through their decrepit doors as *a man* in the prime of his life; I gripped the key as a pledge, and with the dark deliberation of one who has passed his zenith I had to take my seat at the head of the table between the decimated ranks whom my sealed lips silenced: with an inviting nod, with a calm gesture of my hand like the patriarchal flourish of an owl's pinions, I gave the elders, those lost to decrepitude, permission to begin their meal, and this was strange, but in the order of things. Ah, on such occasions they'd once laid soothing fingers on the child's head to awaken him to his existence...that child had vanished. — Abandoned were the colorful picture books that just yesterday had brought a secret gleam to my eye; scattered were the bright playing cards with their naïve and inscrutable dramas of operatic morality; vanished were the handsome, disinherited youths whom the morning sun helped back on their way after a thousand ramblings in the base smells of the night; destroyed was the magic lantern...

Over was the night that had shrouded me: the day, ascending in the east with its soapy autumn light, would find what was left of me once I finished growing. And even if they recognized me when I entered the apartment, swollen with darkness, my clothes holding all the filth and contamination of the terrain I had struggled through—even if my distinguishing features were still clear...would *I* succeed in making myself known: didn't I myself harbor enough doubt as to my form's immutability? Was there a single description of myself that

I hadn't had to revoke immediately…had to revoke it though I could not correct it? Could I still give myself an account of my appearance? And with what words would I have done so? There was an array of extinguished nouns I sought to bring to life with attributes; I sought to imbue their awful aridity with color, but now I was staring at a parade of masks, at the painted faces of corpses. It was a result of my entry into the adult world: only obfuscating participles could conceal the frailty of the nouns; life's dilettantes, seizing power over their enclaves in a last-minute panic, required shabby clothes to cover their decay. — The things surrounding us were interchangeable…the things' localities were interchangeable, and it was all the same which paths led to those places. The names were random in their inalterability, it made no difference which time a person sojourned in which place, in the shape of which figure made no difference…it was always the same name cloaking the randomness. Evening after evening the radio listed a legion of random things; a murmur no longer fathomable had trickled through the cracks of my door, name after name had crept through the keyholes; they had swarmed in as though neither wall nor roof existed, and they had washed my brain. Bit by bit, point by point, they had covered me minute by minute with banal evidence, with the monotonous, sweeping waves of their naming, and when I'd taken the way back to my dream-trains, when I was encircled by the freight trains of the night, when I flailed between steps, it always seemed possible that I had been among the missing, had lingered among the vanished, among the names that had been deported because of certain interchangeable attributes bound up with their ordinariness like interchangeable steps in fleeting directions, like transgressions, distortions…attributes that could have fit me as well…appendages that the missing persons might have misplaced somewhere, that I had gathered up to finish off my adult life… descriptions that made you end up under the roof of a cattle car.

I had grown increasingly uncertain of my paths. Yet more and more often I was drawn to the scenes of old stories that still seemed unclarified, that I remembered—dimly, obscurely—as though they still involved me. It was a sign of age, I thought, to suddenly recall losses that earlier on—in the insouciance, the restlessness of youth—I would have passed over quickly. Now I was groping in search of losses…the signs were clear: all at once I'd begun hastily changing the goals of my forays…the directions of my forays, since it was impossible to speak of goals. Probably, though, what I sought was one single place…a place from which, back then, I'd felt I was expelled; or I sought it because something of mine was still hidden there—some poignant thing, perhaps willow wands carved into toy sabers, clear signs—or simply because it was a place I couldn't find again or no longer encountered on my way back. It had to lie in a region farther upstream, in a different, uncanny region, one that unsettled me more, if possible, than the environs of the old mill, where I could better describe my unease, or perhaps even explain it. At the same time, the uncanniness of this region lay not least in the pull it exerted on my thoughts. It exceeded even the pull I felt on my way to the mill; this attraction was driven by the old prohibition against roaming the bombed-out industrial complexes that began just outside town and were thought to be dangerous, not just because they were labyrinthine and crumbling; there was a notion that the ruins would be an ideal hiding place for all those who shunned the public eye. And it also seemed that this prohibition's aim was to keep me from finding something buried, from setting foot in the places where we had earned our living, condemned to the margins of society by the filthy, menial, wretched labor that contributed to the self-contempt of our class. Finally, something of my own life was buried there, a fragment of childhood consciousness had dropped into the fog, a fragment of time had slipped through a ghastly slimy pitfall and vanished, and I was suddenly unable to bear its loss...it was as though a sentence had eluded me in an inadvertent pause between two trains of thought, as though from then on I'd been roaming the unspeakable. — The eerie thing about this region was that its intermittently forested expanse was undercut by an immeasurable branching system of disused mines, so that large areas were considered irreclaimable and—apart from a number of abandoned industrial ruins looming into the sky like rocky, storm-swept islands—lay desolate and fallow. — The place I sought was one from which I'd been expelled a second time at some point during my school days, when fits of youthful romanticism led me there. I had avoided it ever since, almost fearfully, in a kind of adolescent sensitivity I'd developed toward reality, and little by little I had thrust aside all thoughts of the place. I recalled how even on my second visit I'd barely found the scene of my expulsion, for in the few years since I'd last seen it, nature had thronged relentlessly onward and made the place almost inaccessible, transforming it into what looked like a vestige of prehistory. If the tangles of wild growth really hid my old ruinous playground, I couldn't tell; it was a late afternoon in fall, and here too I stumbled first upon a railroad line, a stretch of rusty track evidently long unused: ties falling to rot, weeds and burdock flourishing between them, brush and saplings coalescing into a dense thicket against a mass of masonry. I'd been following the tracks—soon hemmed in by hawthorn hedges, tall but ravaged by forces of some kind—for several hundred yards when they ended at a battered buffer intended to halt onward-rolling cars at the foot of a *ramp*: I saw that I stood before the concrete hulk of a platform, part of a former loading station attached to a defunct coal factory of which only fragments still stood, and in whose yards and roofless halls the vegetation had long since seized control.

The vegetation was typical for the area, thriving on leached-out slag and crumbling scrap metal; neither useful nor beautiful, it seemed to have sprung up only to cover the wounds of the terrain… or only—I subjected it to continuous scrutiny—to invade my dreams with the gloomy union of its gray webs and the fog…nightmares that recurred in reality, nightmares in which the matted layer of vegetation concealed a core of indefinable glow; as though in some building deeper in the ruins, where the workers' quarters must have been, a light were still intact…or the shrubs wove to spin into my thoughts a gray net of bristling sorrow…to weave over burning wounds in the delta of my thoughts… to knit over the fact that my strange interest in bad places was an unacknowledged, unclear interest in our origins…because I had not actually experienced the affronts that went with the soil we had sprung from. — On reflection, we were actually exiles. Of course only in the indefinite way in which all our names were sheer hubris…all our names, titles, and nouns. So we were not exiles based on some neat, solid idea, but exiles out of instability…out of ineptitude, ignorance, antisocial tendencies; we hadn't been torn from our roots, we hadn't lost our rights, we were in exile because we'd never had roots or rights; we'd never even sought to find them, perhaps we constantly sought the world's most noxious regions in order to rest in our rootlessness; like gray vegetation, feeding on the ground's nutrients but giving nothing back, we settled in the desolate provinces that were the strongholds of evil, we settled between slag and scrap where we could run riot, rank and uncontested. We had always sought the places of darkness—always the smoke, as others seek the first bright happy memory of childhood—always sought the shunting shadows of transition, ever wary of being recognized, for our lives were but a semilegal affair…and we sought out the most wretched work, in cellars, cesspits, and shafts, lowly nocturnal tasks; we cleansed the blemishes, we scrubbed the slaughterhouses, we licked clean the word of mouth, and with the looks of thieves we pocketed our wages. I must have learned of these things when, in search of what harmonized with me, I was drawn to the town's edge where the rubbish began, or to the villages beyond the town, on the periphery where the town's refuse blossomed, the metastases of industry; there notions of my future reality had burgeoned… they'd been growing for nearly thirty years, and for as many years I'd abandoned my lead soldiers to their hopeless trench war in the flowerpots and gone out late in the day to sully myself with visions of my future.

On one of these forays, I was beaten back with such force that the memory of it remained a mere image, impossible to place in a definite time, impossible to link with definite causes or imperatives; impossible to distinguish whether the image stemmed from a dream or reality: every suggestion of truth was suppressed. I'd been stricken by such nausea, the smell of the goings-on clung so close to me that for a long time I didn't dare go home: I had seen animal cadavers being unloaded, at least I assumed they were animal cadavers; I was blinded by a floodlight's beam that illuminated the loading bay as I peered out from a hidden nook, and I beheld a mere bustle of shadowy uniforms, dragging the creatures from the gaping hold of a filthy cattle car with commands shouted in strained voices; it was done by plunging flashing, dripping iron hooks into the animals' sighing flanks—hooks I'd seen once in a film, dragging bales of cotton across piers—and the animals jerked and spread their unwieldy legs across the platform: pigs, sheep, cows, all in their death agony, or already dead and bloated, unusually large, with bitten tongues protruding from their frothing mouths…a froth that brewed in their bellies and welled from their nostrils to cover the platform with a mush and a slime on which the dark men in rubber boots could barely find their footing and had to drag themselves along, cursing, by sinking their hooks into the inert farting animal corpses…until I saw beast after beast slip into the night beyond the floodlight beam, vanishing down a long, smeared track amid the ruins of the old coal factory, where there was actually still a usable building, deeper down, a brick building only half fallen to ruin, with light still inside it, life still at work behind the half-blind windows nearly overgrown by the silhouettes of unruly vegetation; a light glowed there, and glowed more and more angrily as the cattle car emptied at the platform…now living animals were driven forth, diseased pigs and piglets, rabid with panic, slipping on the glimmering slime left by the corpses and sliding down the incline amid the ruins, squealing in such distress that, before reaching the gate of the brick slaughterhouse, they had to be dispatched with hooks and knives and cleavers.

Germania II, that was what they called this old plant, named after a nearby mine that once supplied the factory with coal to make briquettes, and the ruins were still dignified with that name: *Germania II*, that was what they called the whole woods that concealed the remains of the buildings. When a certain smell fouled the summer nights, when darkness fell and an invisible smolder heated the already-hot air, when the air suddenly grew harder to breathe and heads ducked beneath clouds of heat that seemed divested of all oxygen, when every inadvertent opening of the mouth instantly resulted in barely surmountable nausea, the people of this town pointed to a certain part of the sky—they pointed with both hands, a gesture, to my eye, like a God-fearing obeisance—to a place where snow-white vapor surged over the horizon, and they named its cause: Germania II. — Involuntarily I pictured a color (the pure white of this steam looked too innocent) for the stench that ravaged this region: I saw it rise blue from the smokestacks of that factory complex...like the blue shimmer beneath the milky surface of the stream which I followed on my autumnal forays, which emerged from the woods around Germania II, and whose smell seemed to have leached out during its long semicircular detour around the town by the time I'd fled back through the town's deserted center and encountered it again by the allotment gardens on the other side... though the cool of the autumn air seemed to mute the stench, I thought I tasted a hint of it in the vegetables that flourished in those gardens. My return from the territory of Germania II was such a stampede of revulsion and horror that I charged past our neighborhood, fled to the allotment gardens, crossed them, and ran on along the brook until I had nearly reached the old watermill, the memory of which distracted me, until, unthinking, I found myself in the village beyond it and realized that with the long, dark hours, emptiness and timelessness had descended. Hardly anyone lived in the village anymore, and this immediately menaced me with new visions.

Heading home, I was haunted still, still imagined the unseen glow of stench-infested smoke clouds above me, melted fat dripping from them… Oh, this brew swelled not just from the smokestacks, I'd seen it creeping into the air through broken windows, fuming through cracks and fissures in the walls; even the dark red bricks of the old workers' quarters—the baths, changing rooms, canteens, and common areas—seemed to exhale it; under the rotten roof the toxic organism breathed and throbbed, and I imagined the ingenious perversion whereby this once-hospitable facility now served a new purpose. This hub at the center of the ruins, through whose yards the vegetation voraciously advanced, looked as though it had recently survived an earthquake, or at least the foreshocks of an earthquake yet in store: the building stood askew like a vessel run aground, its bulky prow subsiding, stuck unsteerable and clumsy in the mud whose steaming breakers seemed to have spattered it from top to bottom…and in the jittering hull the boilers were still seething, and around their pounding noise the crenellations of tumbledown towers loomed like crags by the sea, like the battlements of a fort waging permanent war against the balmy summer nights, against the autumn days that swept up, banners flying. — I was forced, as it were, to laboriously transform myself back from these nights, as though I'd grown old at a furious pace, transformed to an age to which I must not acquiesce: there in the grove that hid the deported animals' place of sacrifice, I'd become a witness, made complicit by my knowledge, a participant in some *Thousand-Year Reich* and its history; I was now one of those hardened old men living dreamlessly, I too found my golden locks

covered in the filth that dripped from the ramps...
or possibly I too, were I suddenly to appear at our
front door in this state, would be bludgeoned with
the butt of an ax—a wild, poisoned animal that had
to be put away, out of the light.

One reason for my forays to the far side of
town was the worry over what was to become of
me. In fact I was searching for a place where I'd be
needed: I was entering a critical phase, with grad-
uation drawing near—as though that would mean
the loss of the last mechanism controlling me, I had
come under increasing pressure to make a decision.
How symbolic that the externally imposed worry
about my future should bring me to a place where a
once-clean brook became a conduit for indefinable
effluents and accompanied my path with the odor of
corpses, signaling unmistakably, on into my dazed
nocturnal vigils, the end to which I worried. — For
some time I'd been reading too much, beginning
to sense how quickly over-strong sensations could
lead to a surfeit; a harmonious existence in natural
surroundings, I imagined, would forestall the dull-
ing of my senses. I'd rashly claimed to my relatives

that I wanted to become a gardener: I was thinking of the last chapter of *Candide*, which had an oddly soothing influence on me…though in fact I loathed gardens. Nonetheless, the story's hero seemed worthy of imitation; amid the evil overall state of the world he had discovered for himself and his friends the most tolerable of ills: in the green garden shade they fulfilled their duty to subsist. And probably I was thinking of my tin soldiers too, resting hidden beneath the potted plants, unmolested to the point of immortality in a flood of diffracted light…their metal molded in the weight of their aimless waiting, from which they might be jolted when the moon rose behind the window, sending a fiery shimmer through their chlorophyll screen. — Of course these career aspirations were met with shocked disapproval; in our circles gardening was at most a leisure activity bearing no relation whatsoever to work. As a recourse, I secretly settled on the prospect of becoming a miller, envisioning a watermill; sitting around in a watermill might be even more agreeable than gardening, all the more so if it were a mill like the one east of town, which in my need for stability

I imagined as the impregnable refuge of all vanished things. Where a phalanx of grim willows repulsed any onslaught from our side, where, behind the back of a rankly overgrown railroad embankment, dead poplars loomed in warning, and where—I saw it when I first felt the harsh wind of that last November's last autumn reprieve when there'd be no way back, when the time of evasions would end for good with the last winter of my school years— mounting to greater and greater opacity, an early flour-fine snow billowed from the mist, swirled by the spin of the whirlwinds that began to turn like racing millstones…there I might be safe from un- natural reality, which, though never spoken of, was constantly searching for me. — But I didn't dare even to mention these career plans, any more than I mentioned my forays out in that direction. Rather, I thought it more prudent to hint that during my afternoon and evening absences I was investigating the industrial areas on the edge of town. Anyway— now that the question of the future was being asked at school of all the pupils with no prospect of higher education, with much back and forth about technical aptitudes and impending apprenticeships, with hymns to the security of a productive life spent strengthening our republic, and with endless assessments of qualification opportunities and wage prospects in professions with names whose very sound repelled me—I responded after a brief hesitation that I intended to work at *Germania II*, and that they were prepared to hire me on the basis of my appearance alone, without any further requirements. My answer elicited perturbed silence, despairing shakes of the head, and finally the resigned observation that I had proved, yet again, what a piece of work I was...yet again I'd managed to confound even the most modest expectations of my goodwill; they had to own that I was literally pursuing a path that would take me to the margins of society. I'd soon see, I was told, that by sabotaging their most patient efforts I had set myself inevitably on a track that shunned the light—fine, then; no one would put any stones in my pathway. The long-winded diagnosis relieved me; I really did see myself as one who shunned the light, though the phrase bothered me: they used it because darkness, for them, was a deficiency, because in darkness they no longer saw light…what a dreary life. — Admittedly, I didn't even know the plant's official designation; I had never heard it called anything but the name of the old, long-depleted coal mine, a name that sounded devilishly irrational. No one seemed happy to admit that he worked there: Germania II was the embodiment of all that was dark, slimy, and unwholesome; though above-average wages usually improved a worker's status among his peers, they didn't improve the bad reputations of those who worked there; there'd be good reasons why this particular "firm" paid such good money, everyone always said. All the same, I couldn't find those reasons out, I saw only that the men from Germania II were shunned, and I heard you could tell them by their smell, even from afar, the unmistakable smell of the firm that they could never wash away. — This was all the more surprising since the plant supposedly produced cleaning agents, or at least some base used for cleaning agents. I hit on the idea of discovering the ingredients from which soap was made…I couldn't find out, though I pored over all the encyclopedias I could get my hands on; evidently a bar of soap was such an utterly mundane object that it was ridiculous to inquire about it…the existence of soap was so extraordinarily banal that all the reference books describing its mysterious composition had sunk, completely superfluous, into obscurity…almost like a formula that was taboo… I'd have been willing to bet that not a single person I knew had the faintest notion of the amalgam that produced a unit of the slippery, foaming substance he used every day. Had I asked, they'd surely have mocked me; they could have explained the details of nuclear fission, but soap…what enigmatic medley of obscure secretions was this thing I seized as often as possible so as to be thought clean, fragrant, appetizing? What was it that I smeared on my fingers so as to use those fingers to eat, uncompromised? What was this thing that touched my lips, foaming, stripped the grease from my hair, anointed my anus, and infiltrated my ears with a deafening crackle? — If anyone knew, it would be the workers of Germania II, and I set out in search of them.

Strange: by developing an interest in the

simplest of things, you risked losing your hold on the world...perhaps even vanishing from the world. It was as though even the simple things, if you thought about them long enough, reached deep down into subterranean realms; indeed, as though some fiber of their being were bound to the evil concealed there. Very soon I noted that the workers from Germania II really did shun the light; I never managed to approach one; even how to go about it was a mystery to me, and besides, no one in my small circle of acquaintances knew anything about them, no one had the slightest contact with anyone working in the plant, nor did anyone see a way to make such a contact; it was impossible to learn where one might run into them, and in fact no one even knew where they lived...or how they lived: apparently, like animals, they were identifiable only by their smell, and like animals they knew how to elude their hunters' noses. There had to be an invisible yet distinct boundary between them and ordinary citizens, and I almost thought the earth's surface was that boundary: only rarely did they emerge from their stratum beneath ours, rarely did they ascend, perhaps only at night when the sunlight wouldn't betray them, when their mangy pelt smell merged with the scum-born vapors sinking from the smokestacks of their infernal kitchen into the town's streets. Perhaps they crawled out only to perform their dark work, in night and fog, to stoke the light-shy fires beneath the cauldrons in which, as the irrepressible rumor would have it, animals were rendered to make the fats contained in soap.

It was only later, once I'd become a regular at the bars, that I spotted some of them—first someone waved a hand in their direction, later I thought I recognized them on my own—and saw that they barely differed from other people: except that they always sat alone at their table, or among their own kind, and no one else joined them. I too avoided breaking the evident taboo surrounding them, I too seemed fated, for a long time, not to join their ranks: perhaps, I told myself, anyone could enter their effluvial border zone except me, the drinker, who took in the world solely by way of his irritable stomach walls. From a distance I saw an expression of resignation in the stubborn folds of their immobile faces, an expression through which nothing seemed to break, except perhaps a wrath so unpredictable that the least trifle could provoke it: for its cause was found not here above, but in the stratum below the surface on which ordinary citizens strode, sure and insensate…whereas these men seemed unable to control their own feet, shambling and stumbling through the petty bourgeois sphere that was accustomed to the light, reeling, circling rather than pressing forward, an inarticulate roaming, as if through tides of indecision, on ground without solidity through which the burden of their gaze dripped downward, and the weight of their knowledge dug into the pavement where their shoes stuck fast in decay, in burning dirt…dug still deeper, down past the echo of their shuffling in sand, down past the sigh of their shambling in slime, while up above their brains expired amid the vagrant clouds…their pupils were dark tears, like eyes of polished ebony, as they descended forever downward after their dull thoughts, as, drinking continuously at their table, they tried to write one of their letters, perhaps intending to quit work at last, scratching awkwardly for hours to form the lines of their antiquated script, nodding ponderously in the wake of their incomprehensible constructions, and ants chased each other on the grubby paper amid the baffled blue words that were nothing but curses. And I saw them give up, chaotic in their retreat, quickly spinning out of control again, confused in their gestures, constantly jolted by desperate horror like dreamers waking to shadowbox, forced to go on flailing at swarms of panic-insects, or to wipe out their names, hands slapping the tabletop. Or I saw them make forlorn, uninterpretable gesticulations, toneless tongues aided by waving hands, gurgling as though calling from out of the water; mollusks of inarticulately drifting in-between phonemes darted out from the silence, through the milky swaths of smoke over the bar tables. In the end they seemed to communicate in animal tongues, fleeing from their own language...and their sounds fled like the dark stumblings of sick animals, fled over bones plowed up from leaden earth. Oh stumbling over mass graves, oh stumbling in pale grass over the mass graves, oh reverberation of the pavement covering the mass graves, oh, in a land pieced together from tracts of mass graves, oh land like a beehive of mass graves, land covering the mass graves with philosophies, risen from the ruins over mass graves, over the mass graves of the dictatorship of the proletariat, over the mass graves of Lenin's almighty doctrine, oh over the mass graves of "knowledge is power"… oh over the dark unutterable knowledge of all, oh over the grave of the knowledge of the masses, dark stumbling of words and dark fall of dead vowels snatched like stones from their throats, and snatched from the smoke of their earth: vowel-skulls, consonant-bones, carpus-consonants, pelvis-vowels, knuckle-punctuation, organic multiplications, inorganically transmuted when the headings were underlined. And they wandered onward, with dirt under their nails and pockets full of gold teeth. With phrases in their heads like hooks for uprooting trees, with inkblots on their shirtfronts, and bewildered by the last three orthographic reforms, they passed through the realm of the willows, passed under the masks of the willows, under owls and willows, encircled by the night trains' trajectory, caught in their concentric circles of noise, ghettoized gods, taboo, as certain trees and beasts were taboo in the mantle of their matted bark or pelt...they passed, the vanished: far from me, toward the sallow eastern clouds toward the poplars, ink-birds hanging from the verticals, toward a lifeless village toward a brook past the town toward a strangely shimmering, sometimes almost milky current followed for miles...followed with the long-since crossed-out letters stuffed into the fronts of their shirts, down the brook with those inarticulate fragments of resignation letters, cut off by the bluish blade of a long, straight knife, they passed through the severed terrain of their letters, terrain over which under which there was constant, invisible wandering, onward, martial law of the letters followed now by no one, blitzkrieg commands issued to the hidden long-rotting tin soldiers, firing commands to the spectral armored trains of the lost revolution, cited now by no one, firing commands issued to the conscience, letters in all consciousness and conscience, letters to the willows the elms the poplars the waters, o trees o tree of trees, o great tree grown from the graves for all trees, o great tree named *taboo*, stretching over the fields, reaching over the waters, casting shadows over the towns, shadow-casting over the ants cited between the characters…shadow-casting over the white letters, over the white letters to the conscious and unconscious over the letters to the conscience over the witnesses' letters…letters filled with citations from oblivion, letters to the fellow travelers and executive committees, letters to the executive committees of the conscience, letters to the guilds of scribes who band together, to the bandaged eyes, to the scribes of stillness, to the officers of their committees, shadow-casting…inscribed stillness, casting shadows, oh great tree named taboo, over the tracts of the living and the dead, their boundaries dissolved. Casting shadows over the white letters in the summer glow, oh over the handkerchiefs of stillness: wave goodbye you outposts and officers: *oystrygods gaggin fishygods*!

No one waved to me now, and those I sought had soon vanished again. I was left with a mere image of them, a fantasy I never divulged—not only because the image faded behind the night smell, more pungent as the years passed, which the factory's chimneys exhaled. Presumably I managed several times to have a drink with one or two of the people I sought…an uncanny silence surrounded them, and I yielded to it, unresisting. What I had long since become, I thus became more deeply: just as much of an outsider in this town, in the eyes of the ordinary folks that is, who perhaps already counted me, with an unerring instinct, among those who had eluded me. I resembled them deceptively in the way I went around—breathing like someone unable to find a functional airhole, and stumbling as though my observational techniques were under official scrutiny from everyone in town and I had to safeguard myself on every side. By now I was well acquainted with the few people who were actually shadowing me; to preempt them, I invited them for a beer. Then, when I sensed they wished it, I willingly let loose with elaborate and unjustified defamations of the People's Economy; with satisfaction I perceived the malicious glee they couldn't express openly. I explained, compellingly it seemed, the logic of my nastiest accusations—for instance that the stench so vital to the well-being of the party bosses by now had to be regarded as symptomatic of the soil on which the entire country thrived. Here in this place, I said, the cadaver of the republic has been punctured. That's one reason, I said, why even you lot would be advised to demand better salaries for the hard work you do, and not to wait for better days. It's clear that they won't come: wherever smoke gathers, understandable curiosity becomes a universal phenomenon. — They had taken an interest in me for the very reason the ordinary folks avoided me: fantasies had swelled my head; I went around with a bloated face and moist eyes, constantly bathed in sweat, and my clothing, which I never changed—thus instinctively lingering in the atmosphere my thoughts pursued—gave off emanations suggesting to all who approached me that a desire voiced in my youth had been fulfilled: I was one of the men of Germania II.

My fantasies of these men were mainly fantasies of myself: often, yielding to my reflections, I went off on long tangents; it was as though I had left a river's main channel—losing faith in the direction

of the current, which innocently followed its law—
and advanced onto a side branch that turned out to
be a dead end; at first, my thoughts stagnated and
threatened to seep away...but once I managed to
step back into the original river, I knew that the side
branch's stagnant waters were the same as those of
the main course. They led nowhere, but here their
stagnancy affected their nature, perhaps their den-
sity, perhaps what they expressed, and this suddenly
seemed more essential than the sight of the river,
governed by its tireless forward surge, which had
otherwise absorbed me. Like those standing waters
that, in their weariness and abiding grief, in their
persistence, had grown receptive to poison and refuse, to all the spoilage and decay that darkly loomed
within them, had grown greedy for all that was light
and made their true colors shimmer, and had grown
ripe to produce the smell of their essentiality that
revealed them as the true freshwaters of the deep interior...like these waters, the types of people I sometimes encountered in my hopeless mental deadlocks
most vividly exemplified the disposition that the
state, for better or worse, strove to elicit in human

souls: the essence of those who made a dubious and poorly paid profession of practical denunciation. They had to be seen as the most concrete product of this closed society, a society whose schemes revolved solely around its own survival. And they had grown so consistently selfless, thus so purely identifiable with the system, that they had ceased to do anything but smell…from the inside and the outside, sticking their noses into the inside and the outside…they could get their bearings only by sniffing around, and instinctively they desired a *dead society*, because such a society presented their noses with no distracting stimuli. When their sense of smell expired—generally sooner than was normal, often still in their youth, crucially depending on the extent to which they had managed to stifle all human emotions on the job—they lost their value for society, and usually moved on to become unskilled laborers in marginal enterprises such as Germania II…a more bearable end than they would have dared dream.

So they seemed to have sunk at last to the depths of their essential being, where they were calm and expressionless, all their thoughts and desires seeming to be irretrievably severed from society; there was no reason to think resentfully of bygone days, and likewise all intense pleasures lay behind them: if you were hired at Germania II your past was dead and buried…no one asked about your qualifications; true, criminals were said to be hiding out there, even old SS men and other lowlifes, but there the past counted as little as the future; once they'd faced each other hostile and hate-filled— Germans, Poles, Russians, stateless people, rene- gades…communists and Nazis…the missing men and their pursuers—but here a different darkness cooped them together, the dark swamp that was re- quired for manufacturing soft soap…here was the haven for low-level staff and quasi-staff from the state security service, the burnouts too mediocre to fall victim to great purges.

It seemed I was the ghostly crony of these men alone, until they vanished completely and were taken into the lap of the old rendering plant. I never got that far with Germania II's old-timers; they were nobody's friends, seeming to consort not even with their own kind, though their monologues—either barely audible or pitched at an unnecessary bellow—were aimed at one another, and, so it seemed, had to penetrate fortress walls, even when meant for an enemy within their own selves. Usually only their capricious wrath seemed able to make them say a sentence, half an incoherent sentence, a few words, perhaps in reply to an accusation lying years in the past...sentences like replies to voices from beyond, profane replies, not in the tone of an underling hoping for some justice; wrath and scorn rang shrill in their reproaches, and always, too, their threat to renounce the powers in whose hands they felt themselves to be...to renounce the Beyond, to defy the underworld by chucking the whole thing, to snatch the masks from the shadows' faces: oh, they were implacably aggrieved by the squalor underfoot, by death's awful incompetence, by the disgraceful forbearance in the depths below them, by the bad decisions made from cowardice, by the corruption of the material down there; oh, they cursed the weariness that prevailed there, that rose from the ground's every pore, that had long been dragging at their bones, and long since extended into the weather's dreary drifting, into the sunset, into the morning festering of the woods and ponds when night ended, the night that, in greedy sycophancy, had allied itself with the bankrupt nether regions where the things of the future were decided. Oh, weariness prevailed far across the precincts of society's superstructure; oh, barren resignation prevailed over society's well-greased base, and the soft-soaped, concerned solely with guarding their loot, huddled in the smoke like bleary-eyed birds while a great wave of sleep rolled over all hopes. — Dead land, barren land, the men cried, and their voices carried this weariness far across the territory. Wasteland…sleepland…barren ground!

No, the reasons for their resentment didn't lie in the country's decay, however they might seem to say so. This resentment had grown down below, amid the roots of the anger that the willows' night visages voiced on the riverbank. Their thoughts reached still deeper than the tips of the anchors that held the willows when, bending into the current of weariness, they could barely support themselves, in the nights when the congealment reliquified at their feet, when they barely stood amid the air that surged over all the withered growth: perhaps the thoughts of the men of Germania II knew better what life arose from…and even when they barely stood, they knew better than any other language what absences words were made of, and even when their thoughts barely went upright, they knew more clearly what they too had been chosen from…and Germania II was the place to experience flesh and blood, the unparalleled place to experience the soul…the smell of the soul…the essence of being and time.

It…this essence…had come over a crust of the earth, which was permeated, maybe deep down into unexplored regions, with the substance of its exterminated species. Stratum after stratum, all the species' decay had covered the earth. Particle by particle, extinct matter had seeped through the planet's porous mantle to infiltrate the fire-born rock; for eons of past life, death and putrefaction, atom by atom, had claimed Gaea, the mother, and all that sprang from her bosom was saturated with the urine of dead rats. Grass fed on the fluids of nerve-blessed broods that had perished a thousand years ago—after *vegetating* away their time. Having breathed the last of their plaintive hatred, the vegetating beasts merged with the flora's shaggy pelt and their chromosomes rose into the plants' finest points and pollens...the vapor of their essence ascended along the sun's paths; they were driven once more into the bodies of the beast-shaped clouds, before the storms they abandoned the shadowless azure—and in the evening they rained down like blood upon the earth's mangy epidermis. Stuff of spiders and birds, stuff of lizards and cats, blood of fish, of wolves, of apes: a flickering and shifting, and above that the respiration and rumination of the clouds...how the waters, their waves, rose in protest, how the waves of the earth, how solidity surged, and how the mute plains opened their maws. And how shudders of life surged underfoot as we walked, and how, when we ceased walking, night drew near. The night we knew from the chlorophyll of bilious willow-leaves... that tasted of flesh as all things tasted of flesh in the night. The drinking water in the night tasted of pelts and lice, the fruits in their rough skins tasted of tears, of smoke-stained tears like the roses in the gardens I passed that last morning of my rambling, coming to surrender to the world of humanity: oh, I saw the roses growing on dead animals' excrement. And whenever, afterward, I bent over the page to befoul it with ink, I felt the plains gape open...and I heard the bleached, milled-flat cellulose rustle like foam in crackling resistance to my thoughts, and over the gray paper an empty early day grew bright, whose inevitability I sought to hide with dark blue words...and the plains gaped, sighing, and drank in the shadows, the shadows' residues that fell into the rivers, soapy ash drifted at the bottom of the rivers, drifted, drifted, inarticulate ashen ramblings at the bottom of the waters, wandering over the floor of the forests, ash of the stuff of the organisms, with the voices of the organisms, with the sighing and panting of all creatures, ash roaming the weary plains, and trickling in quakes like the hollow impact of buckling front legs breaking through the forest floor...and sometimes the grinding teeth and the moaning of all creatures, finding no place on the paper, where it was too bright, too bright for the humus of outlying places...too bright for the dark in which the creaking of dead branches resounded like an echo, too bright for the silently listening dark that huddled in the thickets, too bright for me and for the voices of a vanished species.

I'd long since known that a few thoughts sufficed for me to join this vanished species, a few thoughts I'd long had; I needed just once to take them seriously, perhaps not even very seriously, perhaps I just needed to truly seize the tip of one: truly, and at once I'd be on its trail, surrounded by its terrain, captive within the boundaries of its infinitude, encircled by the whole of these thoughts' inescapability; I needed just once to bring them to bear on myself, and I'd be lost to all the world...how it would have swelled, the noise of weariness, and I'd be vanished within it.

I'd long since stopped knowing where I was. I'd long thought I was following the brook's babble, but more and more I lost track of its direction, until I couldn't hear the trickling at all. I had left it behind, it had turned aside, broken off, or had come to a standstill, as though at the end of a dead, barely flowing side branch from which a faint bright mist rose; how often I'd thought the day was dawning before me, but the glow in the east, perhaps the mere reflection of headlights on the horizon, had faded…still, or yet again, the rumble of distant rail-road trains sometimes encircled me, by now so un-real—interrupted by stretches of stillness, as though at some signal it would soon start up again—and so tentative that it rang back like a mere echo from the highest cloudbanks…like a November storm that refused to break; and I walked faster, long since un-certain what side of town I was walking on, for the coal train's embankment refused to appear; instead of entering the swampy terrain I was watching out for, I strayed into drier and drier places, expanses of sand, flat stretches where the grass grew scant and low, and I often thought I was walking on ash: sand and gravel underfoot, in places something like rub-ble, crushed and burned concrete on which my steps made a sharp noise; no, not sharp, dull and rever-berating, as though I were walking through spacious vaults. The area grew more and more desolate, and after a while the path had petered out entirely; I walked more swiftly, swift across a parched, dully

crunching steppe beneath the surges of a tenacious
night like the oppressive night in a memory. New
poplars appeared, I had never seen them before…
before that I'd nearly walked into several piles of
rocky debris, had crossed fragments of pavement,
remnants of access roads, the paving from a yard and
its fallen walls; perhaps I was passing the ruins of
the old watermill, covered by the helpless burgeon-
ing of burrs and bindweed from which came a smell
of ashes, the lifeless smell of ashes over the work of
human hands reverting to nature…the terrain had
waited a long time for the coal it supposedly concealed to be mined, the settlements, the farmyards,
and the scattered villages had been abandoned, but
the mining operation never came…what remained
was a piece of wall with a single window in it, where
the ghostly flag of a curtain fluttered, black against
the orange-red glimmer that shone from the horizon behind the wall… I walked faster and faster,
as though to escape the strange, fiery glow: in it
spindly poplars reared higher and higher, seemed
to lengthen, their goal infinity, infinite weariness…
long after they vanished, their sharp shadows seemed

to rise from the ground in the growing glow of an
inexplicable blaze, stretching thin as black strings
against the smoldering red fog of the horizon they
cleaved, striving upward to an almost unbearable
height. From fear of weakness I'd walked faster
and faster—from dread of succumbing to the
sleep whose weariless waiting I sensed everywhere,
an awful patience that filled the surroundings with
its ungraspable substance, with substanceless forbearance that invaded the night like a tenacious
rumble from an alien atmosphere... I walked faster
and faster for fear of falling to my knees, felled by
the blow of an unconscious past, abandoned, swept
up into the heart of the ever-faster past, transformed into a twisted shadow amid remnants of
walls hidden by an ambush of mist and underbrush.
Now some sort of crumbling concrete blocks re-
posed like crouching primordial creatures amid the
undulating terrain...here, barely penetrable, began
the former industrial areas, vestiges of long-razed
factories whose foundations defied all external im-
pacts...at times I crossed long concrete platforms,
ramps beneath which there had to be cellars and

bunkers, endless cellars where the sound of my steps echoed…at times my foot knocked rubble down through some opening and I heard the dull impact stray at length through the labyrinthine bunkers… and far below me I thought I heard my steps' reverberation; I noticed how slowly I was walking, shuffling, weary, though my steps seemed to multiply in the doubling shafts, and weaker as the rooms receding into the unknown muffled my tread, and I heard that padding noise, strangely incongruent with my stride, peter out down below. — The landscape seemed thunderstruck. But it was something else; a storm, even in refusing to erupt, could not call forth such a stifling haze, instead it was as though some mighty blow had sliced off the roof of the night; the darkness—its dome, beneath which all was abruptly still, a sudden quiet as though steaming substances were covering everything—yawned and blood seemed to well from outer space, coating everything down to the last cranny with the dark veil of its glow. Scattered concrete blocks, like blasted foundations, still reared up black against that glimmer, but they seemed to have suddenly changed their position…some had vanished while others had reappeared, or perhaps the shifting light merely sent their shadows roaming. A gigantic moon rose abruptly from behind swells in the ground, and in that moment there was a vivid view of the boundary that was the alarmingly close horizon. For a short time, no more, the confusion of grasses and thickets furrowed the sphere's rolling orange-red face; then it floated, weightless, as though shot from some invisible muzzle, a few yards above the end of the earth. Then, in the opposite direction, on the far side from the moonrise, enormous swaths of smoke or steam seemed to descend: a heavy, greasy drizzle that covered grasses and stones with a precipitate of tiny oily drops, a turbid, sticky liquor that stifled all movement in the air from the moment it fell; after that the atmospheric pressure sank to its nadir, as though somewhere a vacuum had opened; mute inertia followed. Except that, on the overhanging walls of a ruined factory several stories high—with theatrical immediacy it had loomed from the night along with the sudden full moon—from the uppermost edges, creatures rose; owls or bats fluttered in search of the void, then sank as though in fits of weariness and vanished farther below in darker regions. In the rectangular windows of the ruined wall stark night sky gleamed, clean again, only the highest of those apertures held in one corner the flashing reflection of a star, one last kindred-seeming relic still visible, yet threatening now to fade in the reddish shine of the moon as it drifted almost into the backdrop of the ruins. The old factory's fragment of wall looked like the clawing hand of a giant thrust from the earth, perhaps in a mad attempt to play with the moon's red balloon…but in an instant this hand had been jarred, and froze; the moon, in its relentless flight, moved onward, rising past that monstrous gesture, its light striking the hand from behind and showing its decay, showing its deformity and the gaps where its shield had been breached… the moon, a spherical vessel filled with red-glowing air, rose to unreachable heights and spread its fiery circle wider and wider. Behind the ruin its radiance no longer reached the earth: the ground dropped off, the plain came to an end, and the moonlight sank into a gorge of deceptive depth, where blackness swallowed it.

Down there silence had fallen: a bubbling had faded, a hissing that had come from below, as though a row of glowing boilers had been doused with water—a resounding hiss that had mounted to the clouds, a seething and boiling that howled and thundered down to the depths, a jet of flame sinking a second later into a hole that had spewed one last eruption of incandescent water, froth, cascades of high-flying sparks, several brief volcano-like jolts, a tormented bellow of irreconcilable elements violently forced to flow together, for the earth had gaped open and sucked both fire and water down the narrow maw of a leviathan in whose bowels the substances mingled. Scalded inside, the monster gave a piercing shriek and vomited, furiously spewed embers and steam, boiling rock and congealing water into the heavens, coughed iron and earth over the plain, snorted mud and flaming ash over the grass and bushes scythed all around by its singeing breath…then all this matter surged back in, the leviathan devoured it once and for all, gurgling and growling he stashed it away in the labyrinth of his guts, with filthy wet avalanches he greedily washed it down beyond retrieval, and sucked shattered rock and ripped-up steel down to the outermost ends of his appendices; he digested, fermenting, blew off the excess gases with a hiss; gaping, he swallowed the light still left of the vanishing moon; rain showers, flying in erratically, doused the devastating rumble at the surface of his maw, which was round as a crater.

It had happened this way: one night the earth had gaped open and with a terrible din wiped from its face those old sections of the plant that still operated, hectic and light-shy amid the stronghold of the ruins. — In a broad swath around the town's outskirts and all the nearby villages, the ground was undercut by a vast sprawl of disused shafts where lignite had been mined for generations; the full scale of these ancient tunnels honeycombing the earth's interior had been forgotten over time, and no government office was now aware of their extent; as soon as the province's coal seemed exhausted, the mining authorities had pulled up stakes and abandoned this subterranean legacy to the weather; the shifting bureaucracies of successive power-mad regimes had scattered or absconded with the records and maps of the cavities undercutting the country's treacherous ground...so that no one would find the bodies of the enemies they'd buried in the pits...so that the castles of each new slave-holding system could be erected on thin crusts, just as the powers that be, in their malice, passed on to their sons and daughters the pitfalls they themselves had earned... in a single moment of a single night one pit caved in and swallowed the wrong people.

Like a hotbed of malice and crime afflicting the flesh of this district, one night Germania II and everything in it, alive or already dead, descended straight to Hell. It was as though the earth itself, rising up in one last desperate spasm, had catapulted itself out of a dog-like forbearance, bit open and devoured the glowing ulcer on its skin. There was nothing now but scattered remnants: around the burst collar of the collapsed terrain, rubble and tokens lay strewn like body parts on a battlefield. As with a gesture of erasure, one last low gust from a

fleeing autumn tempest swept the site and cleared
the plain for the brightening horizons…as though
an unexpected spearhead of storm had sliced the
roof from an overheated room and awakened ideas
thought long-defeated. The next day, the radio loud-
speakers and local sections in the papers mumbled
their stifled reports and scattered their blank nouns
and names into the dusty rooms; yesterday's news,
lacking a single breathable swallow of air, and all
words, all nouns settled into the dust in the blurry
rooms, settled with a clatter, audible thanks only to
the other noises' weakness, and they sounded like
the subjects of missing person announcements, described with a sketchy uniformity. And with their
sonorous tinder they spanned the breadth of daily
life, clattering loudly at first, then faint and steady,
like the sound made by a small boy walking down
the street beneath the windows, rhythmically striking together two saber-shaped sticks, obsessive and
monotonous, so that the noise can still be heard
after the child has long since vanished.

Now the hole that had caved into the ground
on the site of the former factory could slowly fill

with water, as had already happened in many other places. The circular maw, several hundred yards across, could metamorphose into one more of the many gleaming, unfathomable eyes that filled the district, sloughs or ponds used as swimming holes, though their treacherous depths made them dangerous, especially for children, again and again claiming lives. Their calm seemed to conceal an ambush, and some were embroidered with uncanny tales; when the eyelids of shadows slid over them in the evening, when the trees and ruins above their beaches immersed green reflections in their cold sinkholes, one wondered if their swirling might resume, wondered when they would change back into whirlpools, sweeping everything away again to descend still deeper into the earth...when the noise of freight trains circled more swiftly along the horizon, when jackdaws and owls in the ruins hopped more cautiously and nervously from window to window, when the moons rolled more swiftly, when the night clouds circled more swiftly beneath the whirl of the stars—and these eyes of water gazed up at them; stoic and resigned they stared out from the landscape, full of a knowledge of times thought buried; wearily they gazed, dark and deep, silent about the struggles that had led to their formation, reflecting wisely on the subterranean ebb of antagonisms; slowly circling they covered up the rage, and their floods covered with enigmatic calm the true names of the dead whose tongue-twisting deformities haunted the missing person reports.

In the underbrush by the shore the shadows lay like molten lead as evening came and the hour of transition began to divest all things of their reality. They hid like snipers, evidently prepared in their immobility to winter among the pools of blood the autumn sun had dripped through the crimson-sick chlorophyll; there these soldiers rested, tense in the shadow-hollows of the sand heaps, as branches hung over the glimmer in their scouting eyes, with the barest tremble unmasking them…they'd long since been warned by the leaves' dying hues, but they no longer saw them; they had gone undiscovered for many winters now, their rigid gazes extinct; like all dead things they'd accustomed themselves to the paralysis of their position. The leaves that fell onto the sand were too sparse to cover them completely; their skin had long since assumed the greenish black of discolored army coats in whose fabric the metal threads had oxidized; in snow dust sent by distant rows of poplars and in the winter's rain that foamed strangely in the sand blasted up from great depths, they'd long since been cemented together with grass, concrete, and gravel, with all the elements of the earth, and with all the dead chaff from the fields; and emerging from the smoke, the wind slowly buried them.

No one knew what these shadows had actually been, no one knew what the lead had been before it was molded into those heavy yet ephemeral figures. No one knew the meaning of the tokens that surrounded the remnants of settlement on the plain, surrounded the ponds' deep watery gazes: bricks fallen from the ruins and heaped in mounds; concrete ramps razed by the work of seasons; railroad tracks that had twisted from their rotten ties and bent into the air, crooked and warped; axles that had rolled into the bushes to rust, resting, draped with leaves as though with inferior laurels…no one knew what they had been in reality. Whether they had been causeless spirit, taking up no space until nouns gave it form at last, a pre-found form to make things people could manipulate and use. And whether the nouns had made off, whether perhaps they had fled, had swum away, or had merely been covered by things foreign to the world of nouns. No one knew what the words had been…they had fled like fish in the milky water, like birds in the mist-veiled air. And no one knew if the shadows in the water had really been fish, whether the invisible footfalls heard in the night were steps that had really been taken. Or were merely the shadows of steps. Shadows of steps along a brook path, shadows of steps returning from a territory covered by weariness, covered by the deranged, directionless trickling of water, by the sibilance of grass in the water, by the clash of the current in the water, and by the snicker of voices in the water, alongside the water that the mist's deranged trickle covered. And over the weary ranging waters lay the smoke, trickling smoke, turbid over things once knowable. Or mist, flooding the sand by the water, covering the summer's shore in fall, the invisible summer, the white weave of the sheets blown from flung-open rooms in which sonorous voices sought sleep. The sleep that was nowhere to be found in the sonorous clatter of steps. No one knew what that clatter was woven from, what it had become after vanishing from the places where it once echoed: knuckle-white echoes, a clatter as of pale peeled willow wands skirmishing in the time laid low, in the resting summers no one knew of. No one knew what the shadows had been…if they were the shadows of the willows, if they were the willows, cast down like archangels by time, turned to shadows in the sand-hollows of the trickling bank where they rotted and moldered, grimaces sinking away, resigned finally to the wind-trickle covering them, covering them and whisperingly exposing them, nothing now but twilit shapes, immobile as masks behind flickering leaves and grass-blades, like scattered fallen infantrymen left behind by their fleeing brigade, laid out to deceive pursuers: corpses behind the barrels of discharged guns, decomposing corpses that went on aiming, staring eastward through their gunsights with dead eyes aimed at the

future, at the motionless remnants of a ruin that no
one knew had once been a watermill...a section of
wall amid the advancing enemy's baffled decay, the
baffled substance of the shadows like negative sun-
spots caught in toppled fence stakes. Or the ruins
had been a different plant entirely, among the brick
towers of a former coal factory, where waxen pools
and dark moors now gleamed: later on no one knew
what had become of the old workers' quarters, the
tiled baths and boiler rooms of the defunct lignite
plant; later on, once the last tons of coal had been
loaded, transported away from Germania II as repa-
rations, bartered away down the ramps of world history in endlessly trundling shipments toward other
territories, leaving behind an empty land. No one
knew what fuel heated the empty land's trickling air
once the black depths beneath the clods were empty,
believed depleted: what precipitation now coated
the window glass, and what roofs those were that
loomed from the soapy mists, and what smeared the
windows that jutted askew from the haze and stared
over swamp and vegetable scums, scum-blackened
windows, gleaming like the grease-filmed waters.

No one wanted to know what smell covered the fields of fat, what smell dripped from the bloated walls, rose through the damaged roofs, and filtered from the riven cellars, from the cellars beyond the cellars, from the cellar rooms covered over by cellar rooms, from the keyholes. What smell flowed with the rivers, and dripped from the transport trains onto the ties, and filled the sunlight and the mildew on the poplars. The dizzying smell whose source no one wanted to know, whose existence no one admitted noticing, even when it fell back to the earth with the rain from some gigantic sink of stench that circled wearily beneath the clouds.

They knew it as though this stench came from the stars, as though the moonshine breathed it out. They knew everything as though it came from above...and they dreamed of it, unconscious beneath their rock-hard armor shells, bedded in the cloying potting soil of their homeland. And none of them knew what to do so as to know. No one knew well enough what was allowed to be known, and no one knew how to know well enough. Waters knew better what they covered, white mists knew what

they wrought, owls, jackdaws, spiders, rats knew…
But No One's clan knew nothing of what all the
world knew. Paper knew…the paper's white sheets,
the empty paper knew the gray of the transitions
in the morning, in the evening, and knew of the
madness in the twilight, downfalls in the dusk, and
burned paper knew extinguished writing: but No
One's knowledge lay like slime beneath the earth's
crusts. Or it lay as bones in the hollowed earth; No
One's knowledge clattered in wooden monotony
against the earth's cranium. – – –

Old rendering plant, starry-studded riverround.
Old rendery beneath the roofs of baffled thoughts,
baffled clatter of old-proved thoughts, old pretend-
ery. Thoughts thought by night, star-studded: old
clattery, the constellations covered. And clouds, old
noise: smoke-brain behind the cloud-brow, windy
roof of cloud racks covering the stars. But below
is the fishes' winding light: like star-script, winding, fallen chirring from the air. Past the corners
of close-huddled houses, past streets, falling faster,
vanished. Vanished in the light-divested river, in the
sunken river, cloud-roofed, fading with these waters

into the night. Into the night of the coal, inscribing the night of the coal with these waters, invisible and whispering, chirring in the murkiness, knowing with the waters, fleeing like the starry-studded taurine river, surging under the roof of the murky cloud-cover, flowing far afield. Flowing far into the fields, sinking, shrinking, old remembery. Old star-chirring script-chirrup, fleeing with fish, fish-stars and fish-script, gleaming through the water-murk, old plagiary. Old mummery, swaying taurine-horned through willow-shadows, subsiding in the level fields: flowing onward underground, old surrendery. Shadow-casting: belowground in tunnels casting water-shadows, old cast-offery. In shafts beneath the earth, in channels, walkways, catacombs: water full of starlight. Old rendery: rivers beneath the roof of the soils…and far and wide the fish followed the current, carried on their migration in the calm currents, in the water catacombs, in the fish catacombs, in the far-branching tree of those waters underground. Past the coal beds of night, past the coral reefs of coal which they alone still knew: fish like bright apparitions. Past the black crystal cathedrals of coal, covered with frozen dead earth: fish like flitting gleams in the dark water-willows underground, in the water-willows filled with star-script. And they dream-swam past the prisms of coal, with the neon script of their swarms over the underground façades of coal, through the cities of coal, over the roofs of coal, half-rooved, unproved and sunken. And out over the shores, the edges of the coal, old resignery, leaves waving over, fish like leaf-fall upon the last tongues of coal, stored in the sands. And on past the high coal beds of bones, winding through tunnels near places of skulls, and passing like shadow and wind over the plantations of skulls underground. And swimming onward through the falling sunbeams of the water's great *laterna magica*. And in a vast circle over sunken mills and gardens, and onward like a vast sunken rushing circle, and once more at night like the ceaseless circulation of lost trains. Old smoke-spewery, old knockery over the underground stone shores, clattering over the ties and the rail jolts, noise-covered willow-fencery, noise of earth-roofed defendery: old rendering plant…old rendery…olrendery…dendery…endery…

And at last past several sunken ruins, past Germania II, where the constellations play on the flood, where the Minotaurs graze.

WOLFGANG HILBIG (1941–2007) was one of the major German writers to emerge in the postwar era. Though raised in East Germany, he proved so troublesome to the authorities that in 1985 he was granted permission to leave to the West. The author of over twenty books, he received virtually all of Germany's major literary prizes, capped by the 2002 Georg Büchner Prize, Germany's highest literary honor.

ISABEL FARGO COLE is a U.S.-born, Berlin-based writer and translator. She is the translator of Wolfgang Hilbig's *The Sleep of the Righteous*, also from Two Lines Press, and *"I"* (Seagull Books, 2015), as well as *The Jew Car* by Franz Fühmann (Seagull Books, 2013), *Among the Bieresch* by Klaus Hoffer (Seagull Books, 2016), and *Gaslight* by Joachim Kalka (NYRB, 2017). She received a prestigious PEN/Heim Translation Fund Grant for her translation of Franz Fühmann's *At the Burning Abyss* (Seagull Books, 2017).